A Guilty Verdict

Two Short Stories from

GEORGE BENTON

A.H. STOCKWELL
PUBLISHERS SINCE 1898

Published in 2023 by
George Benton
in association with
Arthur H Stockwell Ltd
West Wing Studios
Unit 166, The Mall
Luton, Bedfordshire
ahstockwell.co.uk

Contents

The Patricia Ward Mystery

Characters

Patricia Ward	Lady on the Path
Sylvia Ward	Elder Sister
Cyril Tucker	Detective Inspector (Retired)
John	'Sherlock Holmes'
Roy	John's Best Friend
Peter Hawkins	Silver Fox Landlord
Bill Watson	Detective Inspector (Retired)
Smiler Williams	Assistant Undertaker
William Jones	Butcher
Tom	Stable Lad
Toby	Lived in Village His Entire Life
Ned	Cemetery Gardener
Caroline	John's Daughter
Tony	Caroline's Husband
Reece	Tony and Caroline's Son
Pauline	Bed-and-Breakfast Owner
Codie	Roy's Wife (Deceased)
Mrs Wilson	Cedar Cottage
Jenny	Codie's Sister

Chapter One

I sat there listening to the wind rustling the leaves on the trees surrounding this place of sadness – yes, sadness – our loved ones all around, in neat rows decked with lovingly placed flowers. The silence was broken by falling pine-cones bouncing on the path below. How I treasured these moments of memories on my Saturday visits here, thinking about how lucky I had been in my marriage and how lonely I was now.

I was thinking of leaving the old cemetery when I noticed a young lady standing at the bottom of the path. I wondered how she had got there without passing me and settled back on my seat. Slowly she started to walk towards me; she must have noticed me sitting there because she stopped. I waved and she waved back. Little was I to know then that this chance meeting would lead to what lay ahead. I moved to the edge of my seat, hoping that she might join me but on looking up, to my astonishment she had disappeared. Just gone, vanished. I stood up, looking all around, but she was nowhere to be seen. I slumped back into my seat. It seemed ages before I regained my composure. Could I have fallen asleep and dreamed this encounter? The silence was broken by someone calling out 'Good afternoon'. I watched two people walking down the path; one carried a watering can and the other flowers.

Having no reason to rush home, I decided to visit the church nearby. It was pleasantly cool and silent, so different to the hot sunny June outside. Sitting there, I could not believe what had happened earlier – who would believe me? I must have been dreaming. I was not alone in the church; by the altar was a lady arranging flowers and my 'good afternoon' took her completely by surprise.

"Oh, I am sorry to have startled you," I said.

We engaged in conversation discussing flower arranging, the weather and things of past years. Then slowly I steered the subject around to church history, hoping that maybe back in the past something like I had experienced may have occurred.

She had just finished her flower arrangement when she said, "It's Old Ned you need to talk to – he has got so many stories to tell."

I asked how I could meet Old Ned and she told me that he sometimes cut the grass in the old cemetery.

I continued my weekly visits and had my moments of remembering our days together; my enthusiasm for knowledge regarding the 'lady on the path' didn't seem so important anymore. Anyway, who would believe me?

Then, on one such visit, I opened the iron gate and started slowly walking down the long narrow pathway. It was then I noticed grass cuttings on the path and by the side of it. Old Ned must be here somewhere, I thought, and sure enough in the distance I could see a little old man who was raking up the grass. I paused for a moment to give myself time to think.

"Good afternoon, Ned," I said and he looked up in surprise.

"How do you know my name?"

"The lady arranging the floral display in the church told me. You see, Ned, I'm interested in local history and you might be able to help me."

"Aye, there's a lot of history around here," he said.

As he talked, I was surprised at how knowledgeable he was. Then I said, "Ned, I'll be honest with you, when I was seated over there—" I pointed to the seat "—in June this year I saw a young lady walking up this path towards me and then she completely disappeared."

He glanced away, looked down and then took my hand, saying, "Let's sit down."

Chapter Two

It was a quiet and pleasantly warm evening. Pouring myself a drink and relaxing in my favourite armchair, my thoughts went back to earlier that day and the look on Ned's face as I told him of my encounter with the lady on the path.

"I saw her too, sir," said Ned, "but no one believed me. I was locking the cemetery gates one evening and noticed a young lady walking on the path towards me. I looked down to unlock the gate for her but to my surprise she had vanished into thin air."

***

Our stay in Norfolk was coming to an end. Looking around, checking I'd left nothing behind, I made my way to my friend Roy's hotel room.

"It's only me, Roy," I called out. "Have you finished packing?"

"All done, John."

After paying our bill at reception we made our way to the car. I decided not to tell Roy about the woman I had seen in the cemetery.

Sitting there admiring the countryside as we drove along, my thoughts went back to happier days gone by and the holidays we had spent together, Roy and Codie, Pauline and me. How different things were now, with Roy like me now living life alone. My thoughts were interrupted Roy saying, "Let's stop for coffee and petrol."

"Fine by me," I replied.

I must have drifted off to sleep because we were home before I knew it.

"There you are, John," said Roy, placing my suitcase on the doorstep.

"You coming in, Roy?"

He looked up to see my grandson at the window. "No thanks, John, thanks all the same. Remember me to the family. I will give you a ring – all the best!" He then drove off.

What a welcome I had when I arrived home. My daughter Caroline, her husband Tony and their son Reece were there to greet me. Between tea and biscuits, I responded to all their questions: yes the hotel and the weather were fine; yes Reece, we did manage to go fishing and I caught a few mackerel; unfortunately Roy was sea sick. I then handed Reece his present bought on holiday. Knowing he was fond of fossils, I had bought him a fossilised sea-horse. The joy I got from the wonder on his face will stay with me forever.

Looking at her watch was a signal from my daughter that it was time for them to leave. I watched as they made their way to the car. Tony was carrying Reece who was fast asleep, and I thought how lucky I was to have family.

Chapter Three

Roy phoned, inviting me to dinner. It's a pleasant half-hour's drive through the countryside to Roy's place. During the journey I wondered what was on the menu for tonight as Roy loves cooking. He opened the door saying, "Hang your coat in the hall and pour yourself a drink – I will be with you in a minute." Whatever he was cooking smelt good.

Roy entered the room, removed his apron, poured himself a drink and sat down beside me. He glanced at his watch and said that dinner would be ready at eight o'clock.

"Now, Roy," I asked, "what have you been doing since our holiday?"

"Mostly gardening and repairing" he said, "especially that garden seat, the one you broke." We both laughed.

After an excellent meal – he washed up while I did the drying – we had coffee and spoke of old times together. I stopped abruptly when I realised he had fallen into a deep sleep. It was not long before I did the same. On waking, it was a few moments before I realised where I was.

"Good God!" I said, "Is that the time?"

Roy offered me use of the spare room, which I refused as I had a lot to do the following day. We had another coffee before I left.

I was about to leave when Roy said, "hang on – you might find this interesting." He made his way back into the lounge and returned with the local newspaper.

"Yes," he said, "here it is on page six. This must have been when we were both working in Australia – take it with you."

I didn't stop to look at the paper right then, but said my goodbyes and we shook hands. It was a pleasant moonlit night driving through the narrow country lanes on my way home.

Next morning at breakfast I decided to look at the newspaper Roy had given me; after a search I found it on the passenger seat in the car where I realised I had left the window wound down – luckily it had not rained.

Returning to the breakfast table I browsed the pages, a story on page three catching my eye as there were proposed plans for a new golf course nearby. I then reached page six and saw the headline: *Missing Believed Murdered*. I could not believe it because under the headline was a photograph of the lady on the path at the cemetery staring up at me from the page. It went on to say that it was ten years to the day that Patricia Ward from Brookside was reported missing, and that after intensive enquiries over a period of two years the police were no closer to solving the mystery. Chief Inspector Cyril Tucker was quoted as saying that, "One day this crime will be solved and justice will be served."

***

"Now, John," said Roy, "what's been troubling you? You've been miles away when I have been talking to you. There is something on your mind, am I right?"

"Roy, when you gave me the local newspaper do you remember telling me to look at page six?"

"Yes, of course – it was an article about coins, Roman coins. Did you not read it? Ever since I've known you, you've been interested in collecting coins. According to my neighbour, hundreds were found by a local farmer practically in your garden."

"That wasn't the article that caught my eye," I said, and went on to tell him everything that had happened to me.

He looked at the article but remained silent. Eventually he said, "Just forget it – you probably imagined it."

This was not the response I had expected from my old friend.

***

Caroline, Tony and Reece were going away on holiday. She reminded me to pick Reece up from school at three-fifteen as they were busy getting ready for their evening flight.

It was a pleasant afternoon. Entering the playground, I made my way to the long wooden seat and it wasn't long before I was joined by a young lady with a baby in a pram.

"Good afternoon," I said and she nodded back. I then watched a teacher fastening back two large doors. The noise of approaching children gradually increased. I could see Reece in the distance eagerly looking for me. When he spotted me, he ran towards me with an increasing pace. I scooped him up in my arms and he cried, "I love you, Grandad."

When they set off for the airport, Reece was waving from the rear window and I realised that with the family away, life would be very lonely.

I asked Roy if we could meet up at our local, the Red Lion, that evening for dinner. I glanced at my watch as I entered the pub; it was ten past eight. I was greeted by Lucy, the barmaid, carrying a tray of glasses.

"Your friend is in the restaurant," he said.

Nodding my head and lifting my hand in acknowledgement of local acquaintances, I made my way to the restaurant. There seated by the window was Roy.

"Are you OK, John? You sounded a little upset on the phone."

No, it was just seeing my family going away on holiday. I didn't fancy staying in tonight."

It wasn't long before Lucy appeared with her order pad; we ordered bottle of house white followed by trout, mushrooms and boiled potatoes for both of us.

"What are you going to do while the family are away?"

"Roy, do you remember I told you about the 'lady on the path'? It wasn't my imagination – I saw her. There must be a reason, so tomorrow I am going to Brookside."

Stopping on my way to Brookside for petrol, I asked the attendant whether I was on right road.

"Yes, carry on this road then turn right at the crossing," he said.

The right turn at the crossing led onto a tree-lined country lane followed by a valley where a signpost pointed me in the direction of Brookside. Approaching the village, one had to drive over a very old single-lane bridge; whilst waiting for oncoming traffic to clear I could see a few people fishing on the riverbank.

I drove on, passing the village church – a surprisingly small building – and began to ask myself what on earth I was doing. What could I do where others had failed? I decided to find a pub and then return home.

In the distance there was a picture-postcard pub with thatched roof and flowers everywhere.

As I walked in, I was greeted by an old man seated outside who then raised his glass to me. The pub was as interesting inside as it was outside, with low ceilings and large oak beams.

"A pint of your best bitter, landlord," I said.

"That will be our local brew, sir."

I sat down by the roaring fire to enjoy my drink.

"Do you mind if I join you?"

Before I could respond, the old gentleman who I'd met outside was sitting opposite me.

"You will be hot sitting there even in the winter – will you be here for the fishing or the point-to-point?"

Thinking this might be a blessing in disguise, I replied, "Fishing mostly, but I also enjoy watching the point-to-point."

I could see his glass was empty so I made my way to the bar and ordered two pints. The landlord asked my if the old gent was annoying me as he was prone to talk a lot, but I said his company was very enjoyable.

The landlord was correct; he never stopped talking, but there was no mention of the biggest thing that had occurred in the village – murder!

Knowing that I was about to leave, the old gent said, "Fancy another beer, sir?" (artful old bugger). It was then that the landlord came over and asked what I thought of the local brew, which I assured him was excellent.

"Pint on the house next time you visit," he said. "I hope there will be a next time."

Before I could answer, the old man said that I was here for the fishing. The landlord collected our glasses and made his way back to the bar. I shook hands with the old man and waved to the landlord as I left. It was quite warm and there were several people sitting outside. I looked back to admire the flowers and noticed the name of the pub: *The Silver Fox.*

Even though today had achieved very little, I wouldn't give up.

***

"Dad, what's worrying you?" asked Caroline. "Ever since we have been back from our holiday you've been in another world."

I then tried to explain everything – about the lady on the path, the newspaper story and my visit to Brookside village.

"Well, Dad, that's a relief," she said. 'We thought perhaps you had some illness and hadn't told us."

"You see, Caroline, I feel this young lady needs my help."

"Dad, stranger things have happened in this world. If you feel you can get to the bottom of this problem, well go ahead!"

Roy rang and I told him I'd found a lovely pub in the country – The Silver Fox.

"How about dinner there? I'll book for seven o'clock," I said. Roy didn't reply immediately. "You still there, Roy? I'll pick you up at about six – see you then."

I was just about to leave to collect Roy when he phoned to say he couldn't make it after all.

"Something has come up," he said. "It's nothing serious – I hope to see you soon."

I was disappointed, but luckily Caroline rang and asked what I was doing that evening. When she heard it was nothing much, she suggested a meal out – so I'd be going to the Silver Fox after all.

"Well, Tony, what do you think of the place?"

"Very nice."

"Take a look at them oak beams, grandad," said Reece. "They came from Nelson's old ships."

We were joined at this point by the landlord and thanked him for an excellent meal. Young Reece fell asleep on our drive home.

"Did they ever find the missing woman?" asked Tony.

"No," I said.

9

"Caroline tells me you're going to be Sherlock Holmes and solve the mystery."

"You told Tony then?" I asked Caroline.

"I had to, Dad – he was worried about you too."

Chapter Four

I began to realise that I would get nowhere unless I took a bolder approach, so today I thought – rightly or wrongly – that I would put a cat amongst the pigeons.

Luckily for me the old gentleman, whose name was Toby, was sitting outside the pub in the same place as before.

"Same again?" I asked and he nodded in appreciation.

There was a grey-haired lady behind the bar as I ordered two pints of their best bitter.

"You'll have to wait as he is changing the barrel," she said. "I will bring them out to you."

Toby looked surprised that my hands were empty but I explained about the barrel.

The drinks arrived. I was eager to start questioning him but nervous too.

"What have you been up to, Toby, since we last met?"

"Not a lot, sir, nothing exciting. I did work at the stables for a few days – I get the jobs no one wants."

"Toby, this pub – the Silver Fox – wasn't there a horse stabled here with that name?"

"Aye, sir, that was many years ago. Beautiful horse, just like its owner, Miss Patricia."

I wondered if he would continue. I had to seem interested but not overly concerned. After a long silence, he started talking again.

"There were two sisters, sir – she was the youngest. When she disappeared, everyone in the village was under suspicion, even me." He picked up his glass and drank heavily from it. "Mr Tucker did try."

"Who was Mr Tucker?" I asked, though I already knew.

"He was a policeman, sir. I still see him on occasions when he visits Peter Hawkins – that's the landlord of the Silver Fox."

***

Back at Caroline and Tony's house, with a large whisky and a comfortable seat, my thoughts returned to earlier that day. I could not believe my luck; I had the name of the one man that could help me – Mr Cyril Tucker. But why would he help me? He had spent two years trying to find Patricia Ward without success. I must somehow try to arrange a meeting… but how?

The poking in my side was not a dream but Caroline, handing me a cup of tea.

"You'd fallen asleep, Dad," she said.

"I could hear you snoring from the kitchen," said Tony.

"Take no notice of him," said Caroline, laughing.

I watched Caroline take Reece up the stairs to bed, calling 'goodnight Grandad'.

I thought Tony's advice was right: to make a friend of Peter Hawkins and take it from there. I had to laugh on leaving, when Tony called out, "Drive carefully, Mr Holmes."

Chapter Five

I spent several days thinking over Tony's remarks; my only chance of meeting Mr Cyril Tucker was through the landlord of the Silver Fox, Peter Hawkins, and so I called the landlord to see if he could arrange it. I told him about what I'd seen and how I wanted to help.

"Hello, stranger," said Peter Hawkins when I arrived at the pub. I could tell by his face that he was delighted to see me, as three months had passed since I was last there. He pointed out Cyril Tucker; I recognised him from the picture in our local newspaper.

He stood up, shaking my hand and introducing himself.

"I know all about your encounter with Patricia Ward and I can understand your reason for our meeting," he said. "I must say in all my experience in the force I've never come across such a case as this. Now, John, you're not a medium or spiritualist are you?"

I assured Mr Tucker that I was not. I tried to explain to him that there must be a reason for my encounter with Patricia Ward.

After a long silence, Mr Tucker said, "This case has baffled me. I spent two years at Brookside interviewing dozens of villagers but getting nowhere. I'm retired now but I won't give up, I'm damned if I will. Maybe your spiritual experience is a call for help?"

Cyril and I – we were now on first-name terms – became very good friends; he needed me as much as I needed him to get to the bottom of this mystery.

***

"Hello, John," said Roy when I picked up the phone, "how's things going?"

"Roy, I've been ringing and ringing you but you never answer."

"I am in Australia. Remember the water irrigation project we were involved in? Well, I'm here as a consultant. They've been having a few problems. If all goes well I should be back in a couple of weeks."

"See you then – all the best, Roy."

***

It was a cold and frosty morning as I made my way to Brookside and the Silver Fox. I wondered if Toby would be there and, sure enough, there he was seated by the fire. I greeted him on the way to the bar and bought him a pint.

"If you've come to see the gaffer, he's on holiday, sir, for two weeks," he said. "Gone to Italy."

"Toby, it's you I've come to see." He looked quite surprised. "I need your help."

Before I could say anything else he took me completely by surprise.

"It's about Patricia Ward sir, am I right? Old Toby's not daft. You know all those meetings with Mr Tucker, old Toby notices things, and although Mr Tucker has retired he's still determined to solve the mystery."

"The thing is, we need new evidence to reopen the case," I said. "Mr Tucker suggested you, as you know both the village and the people. Will you help?"

"Aye, sir, there is not much that goes on in the village that I don't know about. How can I help?"

I told Toby that Mr Tucker had narrowed it down to three villagers who he felt had an involvement in the young woman's disappearance: the butcher, undertaker and the young stable lad.

"Old Jones, the butcher? No way," said Toby. "I'm surprised he was a suspect. I've known him for years. Why did Mr Tucker suspect him?"

"Apparently he could not account for himself on several occasions."

"Well, William Jones was one for the ladies. Rose was his wife."

"Now, the young lad at the stables – I can't remember his name, Toby. Was it Tom?"

"That's right. Young Tom, lovely lad. He joined the Navy, heart-broken. You say he was a suspect but I say 'no way'. He came to see me when I was working at the stables and told me he was leaving because there were too many memories for him here. Patricia and Tom grew up together and both shared a passion for horses."

"What about Smiler, the so-called assistant undertaker – what can you tell me about him?"

"Nobody had a good word for him, sir. They were sorry when he returned to the village after his parents died. He sold the house and moved to somewhere in Norfolk about two years ago. I knew his father, poor sod. Speak of the devil – don't look up but that's Smiler over there."

I could see a thin-faced man wearing glasses. I watched him disappearing into the distance.

"What more can you tell me about him?"

"Well, he lives in old Mrs Wilson's place – Cedar Cottage. That started a few tongues wagging. You see, she had this old cat, been with her for years and it went missing. Everybody including me tried to find it but with no luck. Then one day out of the blue Smiler turns up holding the cat. She was so grateful that she invited him to stay with her. That's the story of Smiler. I think he found the cat and was keeping it for a reason."

"Is Mrs Wilson still alive today?"

"No, sir, she fell down the stairs and then died."

"Toby, what exactly does Smiler do for a living?"

"He used to work at the stables but he must've said something to Patricia. She told young Tom and he told Smiler to bugger off. Since then I have seen him in the cemetery cutting the grass and when needed he stands in for the undertaker. He used to dig the graves but there's no burial ground remaining now."

"I am grateful for your help – I'm sure Mr Tucker will find your observations most useful."

"Now before I go," I said, "can you think of anything out of the ordinary during Mr Tucker's investigation?"

It was then I noticed Toby glancing down at his empty glass.

"Take your time, Toby," I said, picking up our glasses to buy another pint.

"Yes, there was something I remember, quite a gentleman like yourself, sir, ginger-haired chap and smoked a pipe."

15

My journey home wasn't a pleasant one, I could hear him now, saying 'ginger-haired chap, smoked a pipe'. I knew Cyril Tucker would be keen to hear of Toby's village gossip, hoping that it might lead to something.

I had no doubt that the ginger-haired gentleman was none other than Roy. Surely he was not implicated in any way? Although his reluctance to visit the Silver Fox remained unexplained.

Chapter Six

The snow was falling heavily when I arrived at my daughter's house.

Their next-door neighbour was clearing snow from his drive and called out, "Hello, John – Merry Christmas." I could see young Reece at the window, so there was no need to ring the bell.

"Merry Christmas, Grandad," said Reece. I sat there by their fire and watched Reece undoing his presents, thinking how lucky I was to have a family now I was all alone.

"Another drink, John?" asked Tony.

"No thanks, I'm driving."

"You are not going home tonight but staying here with us," said Caroline.

Next morning, Caroline was busy in the kitchen making breakfast and Tony was in the garden with Reece making a snowman. My thoughts returned to Roy. I was thinking of the letter he had sent me from Australia, saying that he was having a fabulous time and had been staying at the best hotels. Apparently, they had a deadline to meet at Solid Rock.

My thoughts were interrupted.

"Grandad! Come and see my snowman!" Reece grabbed my hand and it wasn't long before we both – me with frozen hands – were engaged in a snowball fight. This ended quickly when Caroline entered the scene, having received a direct hit from a snowball when walking back indoors.

"Am I right, Peter? It is today I'm meeting Cyril, isn't it?"

"Yes," said the landlord. "Cyril said he would be here at about two-thirty."

It wasn't long before Cyril turned up, dead on time.

"Good afternoon, John," he said. "It must be two months since we last met. What's it to be – beer or coffee?"

Over coffee I told him and Peter everything that Toby had said regarding the villagers and his three suspects; he wasn't a bit surprised about Toby's feelings regarding Smiler Williams.

"Now, John, I wanted to see you today anyway," said Cyril. "I've got a problem with my prostate and I am to have an operation next week, so I will be at home resting for a few weeks. I've been going through my notes and it's funny that you mentioned Smiler Williams; he lived at a village in Norfolk by the name of Point End for a couple of years. There are a few things that do not add up. I was wondering if you could spend a few days there and make some discreet enquiries? Find out what he was up to during his two-year stay." Bending down and opening up his bag, he gave me a pair of binoculars. "Take these and pretend you are a bird watcher; that way you will be accepted.

"Now is the season for bird enthusiasts to meet. They stay at a hotel called the Birds Nest and also staying there is a friend of mine, like me he's a retired Inspector, by the name of Bill Watson. He knows you're coming. I hope you don't mind, John. I was going myself but unfortunately it is no longer possible."

***

"Your key, sir," said the receptionist. "Room six, evening meal between six and seven."

I unpacked and made my way to a large window that overlooked the car par., I then decided to take a look round. Locking my door, I walked along the corridor, passing the dining room and the reception hall, and made my way to the lounge.

Sitting by the window sat a man who fitted the description given by Cyril: a tall man with a white beard.

"Mr Watson, I presume," I said as we shook hands and exchanged pleasantries. The waiter appeared and we ordered coffee. We discussed in detail the disappearance of Patricia Ward, Cyril's operation and Smiler's time in Norfolk during which time two young women had been attacked, with one being seriously injured. Both were attacked from behind and no description of the assailant was available; there had also been an identity parade that had proved fruitless. Smiler left Norfolk shortly after the attacks took place.

I asked if the police report contained the details of the women who were attacked, but Bill Watson was unsure if they would still be at the same address as so many years had passed.

I was surprised at how many people there were in the dining room. The waiter found us a table.

"Bill, this hotel was empty when we arrived," I said. "Where have they all come from?"

"They left early this morning, John, to go bird watching."

The waiter took our order, we had an excellent meal and then left and made our way to the lounge.

It was then after a few drinks that Bill said he would be leaving in the morning.

"I wish I could stay longer, John, but I'm in the middle of moving house. We have decided to move nearer to my son in Wales – it should all be settled in the coming week."

After a few more drinks we retired to our rooms and agreed to meet at breakfast, when we exchanged addresses and Bill told me to keep in touch. Back in my room I spent hours going through all the police reports, but they revealed nothing.

Later, making my way to the lounge, I ordered a large whisky and sat there in deep thought. What could I do and how could I make enquiries or question people without police authority? I felt like turning round and going home; it must've been the effects of the whisky. But not long after this, I was outside the address of one of the women who had been attacked. Luckily for me, being near the coast, it was displaying a bed-and-breakfast sign.

"Two nights? That's fine, sir. Let me show you to your room," said the elderly grey-haired lady as she led me up a small flight of stairs.

"Call me Pauline," she said. How strange, I thought, because that was my wife's name.

I spent most of Thursday enjoying the sea front, stopping for a meal before I returned to the guest house.

On my return it was not long before there was a quiet knock on my door; it was Pauline asking if I would like a tea or coffee in the lounge. I sat in a comfortable armchair watching Pauline make the tea.

"Sugar, sir?"

"One please – and do call me John."

She told me all about her late husband, her daughter and grandson. She then walked across the room and took a picture off the sideboard, pointing out her daughter, son-in-law and grandson.

"Do you see them very often, Pauline?"

"Not so much now since they moved away – she didn't want to stay here, too many memories. You see, John, she was attacked one night when coming home from her friend's house. A man grabbed her from behind, her screams made him run off and two months later another woman was attacked, but they never got him. It took my girl years to get over this."

"Did the police have any suspects?"

"They had someone but let him go."

***

Back in my room that night I realised there was nothing I could do by staying there.

***

I parked the car and rang the doorbell. I could hear Reece saying, "Someone's at the door." I could see by Caroline's face that she was surprised to see me.

"Dad, I did not expect you back until Friday. Go through – Tony's in the garden."

I found Tony seated on the patio, it wasn't long before Caroline arrived with tea and biscuits.

"Well, John, how did it go?"

"It didn't, Tony. I got nowhere although I did manage to locate both mothers of the women who were attacked. I am pleased to say that both of those women are now married with families of their own.

"As for Smiler Williams, I did find out that during his two years in Norfolk he had several jobs, one being a porter at the local hotel. During my stay, there was a knock on my door, it was the manager, wanting a word. He was curious, as I had been making enquiries with the staff regarding Smiler Williams. It would appear that Smiler was asked to leave. He denied it but apparently money went missing. So there you are, Tony. I tried but found out no more than Mr Tucker already knew."

"Does this mean that Mr Sherlock Holmes now retires?"

"There is one thing that worries me. Don't tell Caroline, but during my visits to the Silver Fox trying to find out about Patricia Ward's disappearance, Roy's name popped up. This in itself is nothing, but when I have mentioned a visit to the Silver Fox he always finds an excuse for not going and this worries me. Keep this to yourself, Tony."

"John, I'm sure that Roy is not involved."

***

I had made up my mind that I would report my observations in Norfolk to Cyril Tucker and tackle Roy on his reluctance to go to the Silver Fox. My one regret was that I was unable to help my lady on the path.

Entering the lounge of the Silver Fox, I spotted Cyril and Peter. After firm handshakes were exchanged Peter made his way to the bar to get us some drinks.

"Now Cyril," I said, "how are feeling after your op?"

"Fine, John – these things take time but I am feeling OK now. What's the news?"

I could see he was anxiously hoping that something may have surfaced that could help him to reopen the case.

I gave an account of my findings whilst in Norfolk, my meetings with Bill Watson, Smiler William's dismissal from the hotel and the mother's account of their daughter's attacker. Nothing to add to what he already knew.

I could see the disappointment on his face. It was then that Peter arrived with our drinks, remarking that it was just like old times. Although I could not help my lady on the path I realised I had made some very good friends.

Chapter Seven

When I tackled Roy about his reluctance to go to the Silver Fox, he said, "Yes, John, there was a reason. If you remember, Codie suffered very badly from depression. At those times, I could do nothing right, always in the wrong. Now you know that's not like Codie; it was the depression that was changing her. I could not have wished for a better partner.

"Anyway, to cut a long story short, I sent for her sister – Jenny. She stayed with us and we became very close, too close in fact. We used to go the the Silver Fox because I was too well known at the local. We both realised it was wrong and we both loved Codie, so Jenny left. That's why I wasn't keen to visit the Silver Fox – too many memories."

Pouring myself a whisky, I made my way to the garden. I could hear my next-door neighbour cutting his grass. Sitting there in the cool of the evening, my thoughts went back over the past months. I missed the enthusiasm of trying to solve the mystery of Patricia Ward. At least I'd made friends: Cyril Tucker, Bill Watkins, Peter Hawkins and Old Toby.

A light dusting of snow had already covered the ground when I arrived at the cemetery. Opening the iron gate and walking down the long narrow pathway I was surprised to see footprints in the snow. Brushing aside the snow, I sat down on the seat. At the very far end of the narrow pathway I could make out a figure but due to the overhanging trees on this cloudy morning it was difficult to know whether it was a man or a woman walking slowly up the path.

After a few minutes it was evident that a man was walking in my direction; there was no greeting as he passed me. As our eyes met I froze – it was Smiler Williams. I could not believe it!

"Yes, Tony, it's this grave or that one, I'm not sure," I said, pointing at the photograph. "Cyril took full particulars of both graves; that was the start of a full investigation resulting in Smiler Williams being found guilty of the murder of Patricia Ward.

"It was a long, drawn-out trial. Cyril Tucker was called upon many times to give evidence."

It was then that Caroline entered the room with coffee.

"Stay the night, Dad, as it is a long drive home."

I was tired and agreed.

"I will leave you two then."

"Tony, apparently Smiler Williams had been attracted to Patricia Ward for many years. He would visit the stables in the hope of meeting her. She realised this and told Tom, her boyfriend who worked at the stables. He warned Williams off and it worked for a time. Later on he returned on the pretext of buying a horse, but eventually he got the message.

"She still continued to get flowers on her birthday that she thought were from Tom, but there was no name on the card. The message was 'Thinking of you always.'"

"How was she murdered?" asked Tony.

"After all these years it is impossible to say. Smiler never said one word during his trial. It was thought she must have been running away from him when she was struck from behind. They also found evidence proving that he had taken the body home, the reason being he knew of a body in the church Chapel of Rest and being the assistant undertaker at that time he had access to the church and chapel. His plan was to place Patricia in the same coffin as the deceased; she was of small stature, so he could fit both bodies in.

"John, if you had not been at the cemetery at that precise time Williams would have got away with murder," said Tony.

Guilty or Not Guilty

Characters

Peter Baker	Newspaper Reporter
Roger Baker	Peter's Son
Jill Bennett	Reporter
Mary Bennett	Jill's Mother
Inspector Wallace	Hertfordshire Police
Sergeant Rudd	Hertfordshire Police
Inspector Cook	Durham Police
Sergeant Blake	Durham Police
Alan Dates	Taxi Driver
Quinton Obbs	Barrister
Betty Obbs	Quinton's Wife
Bill and Beth	Elderly Couple
Paul Bentley	Business Partner to Thomas Fairfield

The Beginning

June the first, a beautiful sunny morning, the birds singing. Little did I know as I made my way through the leafy pathway what lay in store for me.

"Late again, Jill." The same old greeting.

"It's your clock – it's ten minutes fast" I said, following Mr Baker, my boss, into his office. Papers were sprawled over his desk.

"Now, Jill, I've got just the story for you to cover. It's come to my knowledge that we have an Inspector Wallace, a past associate of mine, who has bought Dove Cottage. He retired some ten years ago. I know garden fetes, women's guilds and our local plays have not been to your liking so I thought maybe interviewing would be right up your street. You're too young to remember, but he's had a colourful life. He put away many villains during his long and distinguished career in the police force – one in particular that I was involved with: the Thomas Fairfield murder.

"I remember Thomas Fairfield," I said. "I remember my father telling me they'd arrested the wrong man."

"I covered that story, Jill, for weeks. It put the *London News* on the map; 1985 I think. Yes, it was 1985. 'Husband of Gloria Fairfield found guilty' – those were the headlines. He still claims his innocence to this day. Make that your main feature and don't forget what I've told you: a good reporter must hold the reader's interest."

"When do you want me to cover this story?"

"Well, now. He has agreed to see you this morning... so off you go!"

I rummaged on his desk and found several sheets of paper and a pen that I threw in the wastepaper basket, together with several other pens, before I found one that worked.

I left the *Gazette* offices around 9.45 am. I'd always admired Dove Cottage and was surprised it had stayed empty for so long. I undid the wooden gate and made my way along the narrow pathway leading to a rather small but solid front door. I raised the knocker – thud, thud, thud. I stood there admiring the wisteria now coming into bloom. Slowly the heavy cottage door opened. Mr Wallace was nothing like I had imagined. He was tall with rather a large nose.

"And you are Jill Bennett from the *Gazette?*"

"Sir, Mr Baker arranged our meeting."

"Oh, yes, please come in," Wallace remarked on closing the door behind me. "I must oil those hinges. Now, Miss Bennett, on such a beautiful day would you not agree—" he said as he slowly moved across the room, opening the patio doors "—*that's* the place for our interview?"

On the patio was a round white table with two armchairs, two wine glasses and a bottle of wine in an ice bucket. He beckoned me to an armchair and proceeded to pour the wine.

"I must congratulate you on your garden," I said.

"It's not all down to me, my dear. I have a gardener, a chappie who comes once a week to cut the grass and help with the planting."

We started to talk; his career as a young constable, rising through the ranks to Chief Inspector, Jill found fascinating.

***

"Well, how did you get on?" asked Mr Baker back at the office.

I handed him my scribbled notes but could see by the expression on his face that he was disappointed with my interview.

"There's nothing about Thomas Fairfield, nothing."

"Every time I mentioned Thomas Fairfield, he'd change the subject. There's something he's afraid of."

"I'm not surprised, Jill. Never mind, you tried."

"There was one thing that puzzled me. When he was showing me through the lounge to the garden I could not help but notice a photo on the sideboard of a woman of outstanding beauty, but when I was leaving he turned the photo face down. He certainly didn't want me to see it. I have this gut feeling that there's more to this than meets the eye."

"You've not been in this business long enough to have this feeling. I'd like you to keep your interview and the murder of Gloria Fairfield to yourself. We won't be going to print on this, at least for the present. Now, Jill, it's back to women's guilds and church fetes. I realise there's more to you than a pretty face; cover the menial things but in your spare time I have some old cuttings from 1985 regarding Gloria Fairfield's murder. Look through them – you might find something."

I felt sure Mr Baker was involved some way or another with Inspector Wallace.

A week had passed; rose shows, three-legged races and school plays. I had forgotten all about Inspector Wallace until a chance encounter with him in the village.

"Good morning, Miss Bennett. I'm looking forward to your article in the *Gazette*. I hope it will be of interest to your readers," he said.

"I'm sure it will."

With that, he touched his hat and moved off.

Making my way back to the *Gazette* and having time to spare, I decided to rummage through past copies of the paper. The dust! I could not stop sneezing.

"Hello hello, who's got a cold then?" said Mr Baker as he walked through to his office. At last I found the copy I was looking for. On the front page was 'Thomas Fairfield Guilty of Murdering his Wife'. As they led him away he had shouted, "I'm innocent" and there was a photo of Gloria Fairfield, the same photo that Mr Wallace had turned face down in Dove Cottage. I could not believe it. I went on to read, 'Having been found guilty you are to be imprisoned for life for the brutal killing of your wife, Gloria Fairfield'.

I tapped the office door.

"Come in, Jill. Now what can I do for you?"

"Mr Baker, the Thomas Fairfield murder. Take a look at the front page."

"Yes, I remember it well. The *Gazette* did a good job. Couldn't have done better myself."

"That photo. It's the one in Inspector Wallace's lounge."

"But I thought he turned it face down?"

He did, but he left the room to answer the phone and being a woman I had to have a look. It was signed 'All my love, Gloria'.

The long silence was broken by Mr Baker.

"Jill, I was their top reporter on the *London News*. I covered the murder from start to finish. There were many things that just didn't add up, which I am sorry to say I never followed through. I spent more time covering that story than looking after my dear sick wife, Pam. When she needed me I wasn't there. I'd had enough of reporting. Roger was about ten then."

"Your son?"

"He is in Australia now, Jill. We decided to move to the country. Pam settled into country life right from the start. As for me, I became very restless. When the *Gazette* came up for sale, well anyway you know the rest. I wonder, Jill, whether you've put the cat amongst the pigeons."

The Village Garden Open Day

"Have you got everything?"

"I have now," I said, picking up my camera.

"You know it's the garden we are supposed to be photographing. Keep him busy in the garden and I'll take a look at that photo."

"How are you going to get into the lounge?"

"Easy. He's having a garage built at the side of the cottage. Building is now in progress. Hence to photograph his garden we will have to go through into the lounge and out of the patio doors. It's then I'll try and sneak a look at the photo."

We knocked and then waited for several minutes until we heard someone call, "Hang on – he's in the garden." I recognised him right away. It was Ted, our local odds-and-jobs builder. "Do you want to come this way? I'll make room."

"No, just tell him Mr Baker is here for the garden competition photos."

It wasn't long before Inspector Wallace opened the door.

"Good morning, Miss Bennett. Well, I'll be damned," he said with surprise on his face as he recognised Mr Baker. "Peter Baker – I can't believe it". Both men shook hands. "It must be ten years or more. I heard you left the paper when your wife died."

"I'll leave you two men to discuss old times while I take a few garden shots," I said. After several minutes had passed, I called out, "Are you ready, Mr Wallace?"

Peter watched Wallace join me in the garden where I was saying, "I'd like one of you holding the spade."

Having shaken hands and said our farewells, we made our way to the car.

"Did you see the photo?" I asked.

"There was no photo, just an empty frame."

We sat there in the car until I said, "We'll have to move – we are in the way of the dustcart."

With that Mr Baker got out of the car and walked back up the path towards Dove Cottage and picked up the black plastic rubbish bag.

***

"Come on, Jill, help me sort this out."

"What are we looking for?

"You'll know if you find it. He certainly lived well, Jill. Salmon, caviar and Dom Perignon. What's this and this? We are on to something."

I watched him carefully as he pieced together a number of small torn pieces of paper. He had a look of satisfaction on his face.

"There you are – Gloria Fairfield."

"Why after all these years are you still interested in her murder?"

"Why am I still interested? I suppose it's because there were so many unanswered questions during the investigations and trial. And maybe, who knows, yours truly might find the answers. It's funny, Jill, but when you were in the garden, although both Wallace and I were deeply involved in the Gloria case, he never mentioned a word about it. I found that strange, very strange indeed. First he turns the photo over, then he cuts it into small pieces. Why? There's something he's afraid of, Jill. Maybe your dad was right. Could they have arrested the wrong man?"

Things went reasonably well on our reporting of the gardens Open Day. Our front-page coverage of the Mayor and Mayoress presenting the prizes seemed to meet with everyone's approval.

It was a beautiful morning when I arrived at the *Gazette* to be met by Mr Baker saying, "Take a look at this!" He handed me a letter:

Mr Baker,

I read with interest your article in the Gazette regarding Inspector Wallace's colourful police career but was disappointed that there was no mention of the Gloria Fairfield murder.

> I have evidence which I am sure you, as editor, would be only too pleased to come upon regarding that murder. I'm not a rich man but would like to feel secure in my last few years. Hoping that maybe we could come to some arrangement.
>
> Hoping to see you at the Riverside Inn, Kingston-upon-Thames on Monday 30th June at 7.30 p.m..
>
> You don't need a description of me. I will approach you, Mr Baker.
>
> Yours,
>
> A Friend.
>
> PS: Hoping we can keep this between ourselves. Please destroy this letter.

"Well, Jill, what do you think?"

"I'm amazed. You're not going, are you?"

"Of course I'm going. Could be the story of a lifetime."

"How do you know he is not a crank?"

"Jill, the things that have happened since your interview with Wallace—"

He was interrupted by the phone ringing.

"Yes, Mr Baker here... Yes, received your letter this morning. See you on the 30th at 7.30 p.m. There's just one thing... hello... hello? He's rung off! That's him Jill, whoever he is."

***

"Now here's the keys, Jill," said Mr Baker. "Be sure to lock up when you leave. I should be back sometime tomorrow. Now don't worry, I can take care of myself."

At the Police Station

"You say he went to Kingston-upon-Thames on Monday 30th June. It's only Friday 4th July now – four days. Why are you so worried?" asked the police sergeant.

"He said he'd be back on Tuesday, the next day. He has a paper to run, the *Gazette*. I'm sure something is wrong."

"Have you any reason for believing that, Miss Bennett?"

I thought maybe it would be better to keep things to myself. Maybe I was worrying unduly.

"Look, if Mr Baker doesn't turn up after seven days I'll look into it," said the sergeant. "He could have met some old friends and is having the time of his life."

"I do hope you are right."

Thanking the police sergeant on duty, I then made my way home.

***

Back at home, I had washed and was drying my hair when the front doorbell rang. Standing there was a policeman and a policewoman.

"May we come in for a moment, Miss Bennett – it is Miss Bennett, isn't it?"

"Yes, come in."

I knew something was wrong, but what?

"Mr Baker was your employer, I understand from our enquiries. You were very attached to him, I believe. Maybe it would be better if you sat down, Miss Bennett."

"Something's happened, hasn't it? Is he alright?"

"I'm afraid there's been a terrible accident," said the policeman. "He was found by the Thames River Police. It seems he was the worse for drink – they don't suspect foul play. It seems he stumbled, knocked his head and fell into the river. We found your address in his wallet, together with quite a considerable amount of money. There will have to be a post-mortem but we do need your help to identify the body. We understand he has a son in Australia. We have notified the Australian police and they are putting out TV news coverage hoping that he will get the news of his father's death. I'm so sorry to bring you this sad news."

A voice from the top of the stairs called, "Are you alright, Jill?"

"Yes, mother. Nothing to worry about – you go back to bed. I will be up in a minute."

"We'll leave you now, Miss Bennett, but we will call for you tomorrow morning, if that is convenient, to take you to Kingston-upon-Thames mortuary for identification of the body, if that's alright with you."

***

"Are you sure you will be alright, mother?" I asked the next morning.

"Of course I will. What time are they coming for you?"

"They said 9.30 a.m., so they should be here any minute now. There – that's the bell. Now stay in bed and I'll be back about three."

The wiper blades were working overtime to keep the heavy rain off the windscreen. Sitting there in silence, I wondered how I would cope with this morning's ordeal. The silence was broken by the policewoman turning to me from the front passenger seat.

"I'm Police Officer Lottie Bridge," she said. "We are sorry we have to put you through this identification but unfortunately you are the only one present that can help us. We've not heard from Australia – there has been no contact with his son."

The police car slowed down then came to a stop. Through the side windows I could see a notice, 'Mortuary Entrance, Ring for Attention'. The driver got back into the car and within a few moments the two iron gates slowly opened. The rain had stopped and as the gates moved forward I could see through the windscreen a man standing about ten yards in front, wearing a long white coat. Sitting there I could hear the driver saying, "Good morning, Mr Williams, sorry to be so late."

"We are here, Miss Bennett," said Lottie. I do not remember her getting out of the car but there she was holding the car door open, waiting for me to alight. We entered a well-lit but rather cold room.

"Let me introduce myself, Miss Bennett. I'm Mr Williams – this must be quite an ordeal for you. Unfortunately it can't be avoided. Now if you wish, we have a lounge-cum-tearoom which I feel sure will be more comfortable for you."

"If you don't mind Mr Williams, I'd rather do the identification first," I said.

"As you wish, Miss Bennett."

A cold shudder came over me as Lottie and I followed Mr Williams along the corridor; behind us was the police driver. We then entered another well-lit large but cold room; it was then that I realised Lottie had taken hold of my hand.

We gathered around a large table and I could see the outline of a body concealed under a white sheet.

"Now Miss Bennett, take your time. Are you ready for the identification?"

I nodded my head and the sheet was slightly pulled back to reveal the face, at which point the room began to spin.

"Quick, get a chair!" said Mr Williams.

I must have passed out for a few moments but came round to the voice of Lottie offering me a cup of sweet tea.

"That is not Mr Baker," I said.

At Home the Next Day

"Oh Jill, how terrible for you," said mother. "The shock must've been awful. Whatever has happened to Mr Baker?"

"I wish I knew, mother, I wish I knew. I hope I never have to go through another day like yesterday. The police could not believe it. How on earth did he come to be wearing Mr Baker's clothes? I'm hoping that when I go to the office this morning he will greet me with 'You're late.'"

***

I stood there for a minute before putting the key in the office door and sadly realising that Mr Baker was not there. With a deep sigh, I turned the key and opened the door. There were papers all over the floor, opened filing cabinets, and files strewn everywhere. Mr Baker's office door was wide open and it was no different in there. I stood his toppled office chair up and just sat at his desk. I could not believe my eyes. Why? What was happening? Who could do this? Tears began to fill my eyes. I rested my head on the desk and wept; I felt so lonely.

"Hello there," said a voice.

I slowly raised my head at the same time as grasping for a tissue.

"Hello, Jill, remember me? I arrived this morning."

It was Roger, Mr Baker's son.

"I've been to the police station and they told me that I might find you at the *Gazette*, but what's happened here?"

It took us the best part of two hours to get some sort of order back into the office, during which time – with a few more tears – I relived the past few days. Roger had heard about his father's death from a friend and found the Australian police's version of events hard to accept.

"Dad drunk? No way," he said, "and this – someone's been looking for something, Jill, but what?"

"The letter."

"What letter?"

"The letter your father received." I quickly looked in my handbag and handed the letter to Roger. I watched his puzzled face as he read it.

"It's something to do with Gloria Fairfield's murder and you think this has something to do with Dad's disappearance?"

"Yes I do, but what?"

"It's a good job, Jill, that you kept this letter and didn't destroy it."

"Your father gave it to me saying 'keep this in a safe place.'"

"Why Kingston-upon-Thames and why sign it 'a friend'?" asked Roger. "It's not generally known but my father was a top journalist; he covered many sensational stories. After mother died he gave all that up – he felt guilty for not spending more time with her. After a few years he bought the *Gazette*. When I finished university, I worked with Dad for about two years and it broke his heart when I said I wanted to go to Australia. I remember the day I walked out – that was the day you came in for an interview. There's not much I don't know about you, Jill. In Dad's letters he was always singing your praises. He said you had the makings of a good reporter. You had that gut feeling; he was always on about you."

He handed me a tissue when he saw my eyes filling with tears.

"Look, Jill, I've got to book into a hotel somewhere and report to the police."

"We have a spare room," I said. "You're welcome to stay with me and my mother while the police are trying to sort out the Kingston mystery."

***

"Look, Jill I've been thinking," said Roger the next morning at the breakfast table. "I still know enough to get by. I was wondering if with your help, we could get the *Gazette* back on to the streets? You see, I feel I'm needed here. I'm worried – it's not like Dad not to get in touch. Maybe there's an explanation for all of this. I don't know but if there is, I intend to find out."

The coming days were hectic; it seemed strange with no Mr Baker but I found Roger easy to work with. I could see the worried look on his face each morning as he rushed through the mail hoping for news of his father.

"Jill, what's this?"

I turned round and with his tall frame silhouetted in the doorway saw he was holding a large bag.

"Oh, I'd forgotten – that's your dad's clothes."

"They didn't need them for forensic examination?"

"Apparently not."

I watched Roger make a thorough search of the pockets and lining: nothing. I carried on typing but was interrupted by Roger calling, "The hat – was there a trilby?"

Yes, it's here." I handed Roger the battered old trilby and watched as he ran his fingers around the inside band of his father's hat. He unfolded a small slip of paper and thinking aloud said, "Quinton Obbs, Barrister. Does that name mean anything to you, Jill?"

"Quinton Obbs? Yes, he defended Thomas Fairfield at his trial."

"I wonder... Dad had this habit of making a note of something and slipping it inside his hatband."

Reliving the Past

I found it hard to concentrate, hearing Roger on the phone to directory enquiries in the next office.

"Thank you for your help," he was saying, and then, "Chambers Lincoln's Inn, would you? That's so kind of you. You'll ring back later? Thank you."

I addressed the last envelope, closed my eyes and leaned back to relax, only to be startled by the phone ringing. The caller asked for Mr Roger Baker.

"Just a moment. Roger, it's for you."

I could hear him saying, "Yes, thank you so much, I'm sure he will. Thanks again." He put the phone down. "Bingo! Quinton Obbs – I have his address and phone number. He's retired and lives in Dorset."

He dialled again. "Good morning, could I speak to Mr Quinton Obbs please?"

"Speaking."

"I'm sorry to trouble you, sir. I'm Roger Baker of the *Gazette* and I was wondering if—"

"I'm sorry, I am not available." And with that, the phone went dead.

Looking up I could see the disappointment on Roger's face as he stood in the doorway.

"I didn't handle that too well, Jill."

The hours passed with a hardly a word being spoken. At ten to six, we decided to call it a day. I turned the key in the door, locking up for the night, when I heard the phone ringing.

"Don't bother Jill, they'll have to ring back tomorrow."

"No, it might be important." I unlocked the door.

"You or me?" asked Roger.

"You answer it."

"Hello, Roger Baker, can I help you?" With one hand over the mouthpiece he whispered, "It's Quinton Obbs." I picked up the other phone and heard him say, "You did say your name was Roger Baker? Are you related to Peter Baker, once of the *London News?*"

"Yes, sir, I am his son. It's about Dad that I rang you. My father had this habit of slipping notes inside his trilby hatband. That's where I found your name. I was hoping you might shed some light on his disappearance."

"You say your father's disappeared? I don't know how I can help you – it must be ten or eleven years since I last saw him. He was a true friend to me in my hour of need. If there's anything I can do to help... anything."

***

"So, you're Peter's son and this young lady is your wife?" said Quinton Obbs, gesturing to me.

"No, sir, this is Jill. She works for the *Gazette*, my father's paper."

"Oh forgive me, please do come in."

As we entered a large oak-panelled room we were met by a large golden retriever who decided I would be the one to pamper him.

"He loves all that – please be seated," said Obbs.

At that moment a middle-aged woman with a round pleasant face entered the room.

"Barbara, this young lady is Jill and this is Peter Baker's son. Remember Peter, my dear"?

"Yes, indeed I do. Quinse tells me your father has disappeared."

"Yes, we are desperately worried," said Roger. "You see, things have happened that we can't understand. It's unlike Dad not to get in touch. It's a mystery. I was in Australia when the police got in touch with me and told me the terrible news that my father had drowned in the Thames. Jill had the terrifying experience of identifying the body."

"But you say your father has disappeared – I don't understand," said Obbs.

"You see, the body wasn't that of my father. He was wearing my father's coat and the inside pocket contained my father's wallet, so the police assumed it was Dad."

"Barbara, I think coffee is called for. These two young people have had quite a long journey."

"Oh, I'm so sorry – of course, coffee."

Quinton Obbs listened intently as I retold every small detail – the interview with Inspector Wallace, the face-down photo of Mrs Fairfield, that same photo torn into pieces, his reluctance to discuss the Fairfield murder, the mystery phone call to Roger's father, the arranged meeting at Kingston-upon-Thames, the police requiring me to identify the body and the *Gazette* office turned over. Roger sensed by their glances that when I mentioned Inspector Wallace and the Fairfield Murder it had an effect on both Mr and Mrs Obbs. When I had finished reliving the past few weeks there was quite a long silence, during which Barbara collected the coffee cups, placed them on the tray and left the room.

When she returned she sat down and looked across at her husband.

"Now, Roger, what I am about to tell you must go no further than this room," said Obbs. "Do I have your promise on that?"

"I give you my word of honour, sir, not one word will I repeat."

"I defended Thomas Fairfield and hearing those names again – Inspector Wallace and Mrs Fairfield – brings back a time in my life that became a nightmare. Your father was a great help to me during that time. My investigations led me to believe that Thomas was innocent, completely innocent of the crime he was accused of. Not only did I think him innocent but so did Inspector Wallace. I had an open-and-shut case."

He got up and walked to a large selection of books behind him. Sliding the bookcase glass open, he selected a book and took from the centre page a photograph. The expression on his face showed signs of anger as he looked at it.

"This photo, Roger, ruined me and put an innocent man in prison for life." He then handed me the photo; although a few years had passed there was no mistaking the fact that Quinton Obbs was the man in the photograph. Roger could not believe his eyes: there was

Obbs – an eminent barrister – in bed, totally naked, lying between two girls… who were *also* naked.

"Can you imagine if this got into the papers? 'Eminent barrister in sex scandal'? The powers that be at that time suppressed the story on condition that I gave up defending Thomas Fairfield. I had no option but to retire. They wanted Thomas Fairfield to be found guilty. Why? They had their reasons. Who those two girls were, I haven't a clue; I was set up. All I remember was that night I had a phone call to meet an important witness in that hotel. I'd had one drink. It must have been doped because I don't remember a thing after that. They went to a lot of trouble to get me off the case – why, is a mystery to me. I'm not surprised your father was interested when he found out Inspector Wallace had moved nearby. Wallace, your father and I were closely involved; it was your father that gave me that photo. How he got hold of it, I don't know. He came to me and listened to my side of the story. He was determined to find out the truth behind my set-up and promised he would not print the photo. It was then that your mother became ill – your dad was heartbroken when she died and that was the last time I saw him. I heard he began drinking heavily and lost all interest."

"Yes, I'm afraid he did," said Roger. "I was about ten when we moved to the country. The *Gazette* came on the market and I'm pleased to say Dad bought it. He began to take interest again. When I left university I worked with Dad for about two years before going to Australia. Mr Obbs, I appreciate your time and realise that reliving the terrible experience you went through and how it ruined your career is very difficult."

"Roger, it nearly ruined my marriage too," he said as he placed his hand on his wife's hand and gave it a gentle squeeze.

"Mr Obbs, why go to all that trouble to blackmail you? There must be something they're afraid of."

I broke the long silence.

"Roger's father's disappearance, Inspector Wallace, Mrs Fairfield's murder and your own terrible experience… surely these are all linked together in some way. As his barrister at the time, you said you thought that Thomas Fairfield was innocent. What made you think that?"

"The more I saw him, the more I felt him to be innocent of the crime he was charged with. I remember our first meeting. He told me he thought his wife and business partner were having an affair and it seems he wasn't the first, but one of many. It seems she entertained quite a few gentleman friends. I felt sorry for him – not only was his wife carrying on, but his partner was robbing him thick and thin."

Both Quinton and Barbara waved to us as we drove away.

"You're quiet, Jill."

"I realise now how very involved your dad was – I had no idea. I understand now his visit to Kingston. Whatever could have happened?"

"I wish I knew," said Roger. "I have a feeling there's more to this than we realise."

Departure for Newcastle

1st August, 1985

She felt the early morning chill. Standing in the doorway, she watched him walk towards the garage and heard the up-and-over sound switch as he drove out and the garage doors closed behind him. He stopped and lowered his driver's side window.

"Gloria, let's see. Today's Monday. I should be back by Wednesday."

"Drive carefully, darling," she said, watching him slowly drive off.

***

"He's just left," said Gloria. "Did you know he's calling in at the office before driving to Newcastle?"

"Yes, I knew. He rang me last night. When can I see you?"

"Not today, Paul. Tomorrow at the hotel."

"Why not today? Please, Gloria."

"I'm sorry, Paul, I can't make it today. See you tomorrow for lunch. So until then, darling, goodbye."

***

"You're sure these figures are up to date, Paul?" asked Thomas at the office. "Looks a bit high, pricewise."

"I've checked them against your specifications and they're correct."

"OK. The time is now 9.15 – if I leave now I should arrive about 2.30, with a stop for lunch. Now my appointment on site is at 3.30. That's OK – plenty of time. I'll be off now, Paul."

"Pleasant journey, Thomas."

Thomas felt relaxed away from the pressures of work and demands from Gloria. He listened to the car radio and thought how he needed this break. Mile after mile passed until he saw 'Services Two Miles Ahead – Tea and Sandwiches'.

He pulled over and went into the café.

"Is this anyone's seat?" asked a young man who had come up to the table where Thomas was sitting.

"No, please do."

He could've done without conversation, but that wasn't to be. His young table companion never stopped talking and seemed to go from one subject to another.

"Where are you off to then, Newcastle? Any chance of a lift?"

"You've no car then?"

"No, I got a lift from London."

Reluctantly Thomas agreed to take him as far as Durham, which was on his way. Looking at his watch, he could see he had some lost time to make up. For once his passenger had stopped talking until he said, "What do you think, guv? Interested?" Looking down, Thomas could see a ladies' diamond necklace in the man's hand.

"It's not stolen is it?"

"No, Guv'nor, it was my girlfriend's, cost me a fortune. I wasn't going to let her keep it, the way she treated me. Fifty pounds. What do you say? The case is worth that."

"OK," said Thomas. "I'll give you the money when we arrive in Durham. With that the young man slipped the case into Thomas' pocket. His voice was beginning to get on Thomas' nerves. He wasn't really interested but it seemed the young man had had a quarrel with his girlfriend about her friendship with another man and took back his necklace. For a moment or two he enjoyed the silence from his voice until it rang out again, "Beautiful car, guv. Do you always travel this fast?"

"Usually." That was a lie – he simply wanted to unload his passenger as quickly as possible.

"Look out!" shouted the young man.

***

"It happened so quick, officer. He overtook at a terrific speed, went into a spin, veered off the road, and overturned several times before bursting into flames. There was nothing we could do."

"It was a deer, Dad. It ran in front of the car – I saw it."

"I never saw the deer, officer, but he certainly did try to avoid something."

"I will need your name and address, sir. Can you add anything more to your statement?"

"No, officer."

***

"Looks a bad one, Blake," said Inspector Cook of Durham Police arriving at the scene.

"Yes, sir. They've extinguished the fire. Just one passenger burnt to a cinder."

"Any idea who he is?"

"I hope the car registration will tell us. Excuse me, sir," he said as his mobile phone rang. "Yes. You have? Good. It's a Thomas Fairfield."

***

"What's the latest on the burn-out, Blake?" asked Inspector Cook back at the local Police Station.

"The car, or what remains of it, sir, is at the local garage. We are waiting on that report. Mr Thomas Fairfield's remains are now at the mortuary but identification is going to be a problem. I'm now waiting to hear from Mrs Fairfield."

"I hope you told the officers to break the news gently and you have the address of those roadside witnesses."

"Yes, sir."

"OK, I'll leave it to you then."

Only a few moments had passed when Police Constable Blake was knocking on the Superintendent's office door.

"Come in. Oh it's you, Blake."

"Sir, I've just had news from the Hertfordshire police that our Mr Thomas Fairfield could be a murderer and that Inspector Wallace is on his way to see you."

Taking Bruce for a Walk

"My feet are killing me," said Beth. "What a relief to sit down. You can let Bruce off the lead now, Bill. I do enjoy our morning stroll – it's so lovely here. Hello, Bruce has found a friend. That young man does not look right to me."

"Oh, there you go again," said Bill. "He looks as though he's been out all night."

"He probably has."

"I'm going over," said Bill.

She watched her husband walking on the grass towards where the young man was sitting.

"He's taken a shine to you, he loves all that fuss," said Bill. "Are you alright? You're not ill, are you?"

"No, just confused. What's the name of this place?"

"It's Markham Common. Are you sure you're alright?"

"What day is it?"

"Today's Tuesday 2nd August. That's a nasty bruise you have on the side of your face." Bill quickly attached the lead to Bruce's collar. "Now, you're sure you're alright?"

"Yes, thank you."

The young man watched the couple disappear into the distance and said, thinking aloud, "Markham Common. Tuesday. How did I get here? Who am I?" He looked at the necklace he had taken from his pocket and he had no idea who he was.

***

Looking up from his desk, Inspector Cook saw a tall rather lean man standing in the doorway.

"Inspector Wallace? I hope you had a pleasant journey. Sit yourself down. Tea or coffee?"

"Coffee please." Wallace felt at ease speaking to Inspector Cook. There was no resentment from him about working on his patch.

"You've got the address of the roadside witness?" asked Cook.

"Yes, thank you," said Wallace. "So he lost control at what you estimate was between eighty and ninety miles per hour, skidded, spun off the road and overturned several times before bursting into flames. Impossible to identify the driver's body as the clothing was burnt to a cinder. I see you moved the car to the local garage. That's a pity."

"To us it was just a road traffic accident and not a murder enquiry."

"Yes I understand. Now is there anything not in this report that you'd like to tell me?"

"No, I don't think so. Would you be good enough to drive me to the mortuary and would it be possible to see the pathologist there?"

On their arrival at the mortuary both officers were greeted by Dr Rose Brown.

"I'm sorry, Inspector Wallace," she said. "I'm unable to help you in your enquiries but as you can see the body, clothes and everything were burnt to a cinder. It was only the car registration number we had to go on. There was one thing – his shoes melted in the heat but one sole was welded to his foot. Here you are." She handed Inspector Wallace a plastic bag containing the sole.

"What size would this be, Dr Brown?"

"He had rather a small foot for a man of six feet six inches."

"Thanks for all your help. If anything else turns up, give me or Inspector Cook a ring."

∗∗

"I'd like to thank you for all your help, also for the coffee," said Wallace, back at the Police Station. "Now, before I leave, may I use your phone?"

"By all means."

"Hello, put me through to Sergeant Rudd. It's Inspector Wallace here."

"Hello, sir, how's things?"

"I'm just about to leave but I want you to find out Thomas Fairfield's shoe size."

"His shoe size? I'll get onto that right away, sir."

He arrived back at his station about 8.15 p.m.

"Any luck, Ruddy?"

"Yes sir. Size nine and a half."

"So if that wasn't Thomas Fairfield, who was it then?"

"Pardon, sir?"

"Only thinking aloud, sergeant."

***

"Janette, please could you put a call through to Inspector Cook? You have the number."

"Yes, sir."

"I'll take the call in my office. Hello, Inspector Cook? Good morning and how are you?"

"Very well, thank you, apart from the rain – it's pouring here."

"I have reason to believe Thomas Fairfield wasn't travelling alone. Someone else was in that car at the time of the accident. It's possible that those charred remains were his passenger's, not Thomas Fairfield's. I believe our Mr Fairfield is out there somewhere, having been thrown clear of the accident. I've managed to get hold of Fairfield's latest photo, which you should receive sometime today. I'd like you to issue it to your local press. Also check the local hospitals and medical centres because he could be in need of medical attention."

***

"Well I'll be. Beth, look at this." Bill handed the morning paper across the breakfast table. "It's him, the man on the common."

She then read aloud, "Have you seen this man? Today police released this photo of Thomas Fairfield suspected of killing his wife."

The Murder Scene

"Who discovered the body?" asked Inspector Wallace.

"A Paul Bentley, Mrs Fairfield's husband's business partner. Apparently they had arranged to meet on Tuesday at the Claremont Hotel. When she never arrived, after phoning several times he called at the house. Apparently they had often stayed at the Claremont Hotel, according to the manager, as Mr and Mrs Smith."

"Have you checked the neighbours?"

"Yes, sir. According to the next-door neighbour, a Miss Williams, it was no surprise to her, the way Mrs Fairfield carried on. She always knew when Mr Fairfield was away on business, because the wife's men friends would arrive."

"Our Mrs Fairfield seems to have been quite a busy young lady."

"Yes, sir. It's the bedroom at the top of the stairs, first door on the right".

"Good morning, Wallace," said the SOCO (Scenes of Crime Officer) photographer. "I've nearly finished. A few more angle shots and that's me done. I would say she's been dead about twenty-four hours, strangled."

Wallace glanced around the room before looking down at Mrs Fairfield lying on the bed in a black negligee.

"What a waste of a young life."

"You can say that again, Wallace. I'll have these ready by tomorrow. Is that OK?"

"Yes, fine."

Finding himself alone in the room, he went to the bedroom window and pulled the curtains apart. He could see a large square grassed area with big detached executive houses around it. It never registered at first but then he caught sight of it again in one of the houses opposite; in a downstairs room there was a bulb flash and then another. He closed the door behind him and went downstairs and watched the SOCO photographer drive away. He then spoke to the young constable on duty outside the house.

"When your relief arrives, I want you to find out who lives there," he said, pointing to the house directly opposite. "He or she is interested in photography. Find out all you can, lad, and report to me personally."

"Very good, sir."

Wallace had been back at his office about half an hour and was enjoying a cup of tea when the phone rang.

"Inspector Cook here. You were right, guess who walks into our village police station? None other than Thomas Fairfield! Recognised himself by the press photo. Claims to have lost his memory and has no idea who he is. He's in custody here. What do you want me to do?"

"This loss of memory – is it genuine?"

"Yes, I think it is."

"I'd like you to hold him for a week or so. That will give time to put things in place this end. Is that OK with you?"

"Yes, no problem."

He put down the phone and there was a knock on his office door.

"There's a Mr Quinton Obbs to see you, sir."

"Oh, yes, show him in."

"Good morning, Inspector," said Obbs. "First let me introduce myself. I'm Quinton Obbs, barrister defending Mr Fairfield."

"Mr Obbs, as I said on the phone, there's not much I can tell you so early on in my investigations, your client it seems being miles away at the time of the murder."

"This loss of memory you believe to be true? Am I right, Inspector? Also that a witness has come forward who saw him at the service area?"

"Yes, a lady remembers this rather shabby young man joining the table of this well-dressed man at about the time of the murder – she now recognises him from the newspapers as Thomas Fairfield."

"I assume this young man she describes is the one involved in the accident, Inspector Wallace. Off the record, do you think Thomas Fairfield killed his wife?"

"Off the record – no."

"Inspector, during your investigations you must like myself have found out about her affairs with men friends?"

"More like clients, I'd say."

"Do you think Thomas knew?"

"I don't know. Maybe. I've questioned Fairfield's close associates. Gloria Fairfield's men friends – each and every one questioned – could account for themselves at the time of the murder. I've got nothing to go on at present and if you find out anything that might help my investigation…" At that point he was interrupted by the ringing of the phone. "Excuse me. Hello, Inspector Wallace here. Good God, is that the time? I'm on my way."

"I can see you're a busy man, Inspector. Thank you for seeing me. I do appreciate it."

That was one of many meetings over the coming months.

∗∗∗

"I'll go, dear," said Quinton.

"Good morning, postie. Fine morning."

"Yes, sir."

"Where do I sign?"

"Just there."

"Any for me, Quinse?"

"No, just one registered letter for me… I don't believe it."

"What's wrong?"

"They're taking me off the case."

"They're what?"

"Taking me off the case. No reason – listen to this:

Brown Obbs, Barristers of Law

Dear Quinton,

Bring all relevant information regarding the Thomas Fairfield brief to the office on Monday the 15th of August. You will no longer represent him in the forthcoming trial.

Yours,

D Brown

Quinton rushed to the office.

"What's all this about? I've no intention of giving up this case. I can prove my client is innocent."

"Look, Quinton, I'm as upset as you are. I understand how you feel being taken off this case after all the hard work it has involved but I'm afraid it wasn't my decision."

"Not your decision? I don't understand."

"Look, old boy, don't upset yourself. There's going to be a retrial and Derick Upson will take over.

"Whose idea is that? I can tell you now, whoever's decision it was, I'm staying with the case."

Obbs

16ᵗʰ August, 1985

It was late afternoon when Obbs arrived, passing several familiar faces as he made his way to Inspector Wallace's office. Wallace must have seen Obbs through the glass partition. He quickly opened then closed the door behind Obbs as he entered the room.

"Is it true? They've taken you off the case?"

How on earth did he know? Before Obbs could answer, Wallace said, "I think I know why."

Obbs watched him nervously fumbling through the papers on his desk before coming across a large brown envelope.

"Now what I am about to tell you," he said, "I want your promise that it will be between us. Do you agree?"

"Yes of course."

"I was looking out of the window of Gloria Fairfield's bedroom when I noticed several photo flashes from the house directly opposite. Having agreed to attend a student's prize-giving that morning, I gave the task of looking into this to a young constable. He questioned the occupant and confiscated the camera and films and I've had the films developed. The constable reported that the occupant was a retired dentist of about seventy-two who had always been interested in photography."

Wallace picked up an envelope and handed it to Obbs across the desk, "Now take your time and study the photographs carefully."

The peeping tom certainly had a good camera. The details were so clear and even the date was embossed on them. The first photo showed Thomas Fairfield standing in the open doorway signing for a delivery from the postman. Another was of Gloria Fairfield in her dressing gown waving goodbye to her husband as he drove away. There were several more cars arriving, some chauffeur-driven.

Wallace then pointed to one particular photograph.

"See the date?" he said. "It was taken on the day she was murdered."

It showed Gloria Fairfield still in her dressing gown greeting a rather tall slim man.

"I don't get the connection, said Obbs. "You can only see the back of this man. What's the point? It could be anyone."

"It's the time. Fifteen minutes later when this man left; the same man. Now take a look at this," he said, handing another photo across the desk.

"Good God, I don't believe it."

"How can we continue our enquiries with this new evidence? No wonder they want you off the case. I'm being pressurised from above to charge Thomas Fairfield with the murder of his wife. Someone's worried we might stumble onto something they wish to keep quiet about… and that's not all. I think you are acquainted with a Peter Baker of the *London News*? He informs me that our retired dentist-cum-photographer is none other than a Secret Service Agent who's been, as they say, casing the place for months."

***

Obbs' drive home was a very thoughtful one. What's at the back of this, he kept thinking. Her last visitor… no, surely not. It hardly bore thinking about. If that man was involved it would explain my removal from the case and the pressure on Wallace to return a verdict of guilty. Why should another man pay for someone else's crime?

Being in this frame of mind when Obbs arrived home, he decided to look through his case notes, only to be interrupted by the ringing of the phone.

"It's Brown, dear," said Obbs' wife, "he has been trying to contact you all day."

"Look Quinton, old boy, it wasn't my idea to take you off the case. I've had another call from the Home Office and they want all relevant information relating to the Gloria Fairfield murder and they want it now. So it's up to you, Quinton. You decide what you want to do."

"What time do you expect Mr Baker, Quinse?"

"Sometime this evening."

"He's a newspaper reporter, isn't he? I know he is a friend of yours, but do you think it's wise after what you've been through?"

"Oh yes. I've known Peter for quite a few years. We used to meet in a wine bar after a hectic day to unwind. Poor chap, he's got his troubles too, dear, his wife is very ill."

Obbs was pleased to see Peter again; he needed a friend, especially now.

"It's good to see you, Peter. And your wife – any improvement?"

"I'm afraid not. It's just a matter of time."

"Oh, I'm sorry."

"Quinton, I'm giving up reporting. I've had enough, I'm moving to the country." He stopped suddenly, the sorrow on his face telling a story.

"Now, Peter, the reason for your visit?"

"You retiring and giving up the Thomas Fairfield case; I couldn't believe it. I made a few enquiries. I've many influential friends in high places. I had to twist an arm or two and promise not to put a word in print, but I know now why you retired and about the hotel. When nothing appeared in the press it had to be a set-up, but why?"

"Peter, behind the scenes there's a powerful group of people who run this country called 'The Establishment'. During my investigations, I found out something. As good a friend as you are, Peter, for your own safety I dare not tell you. It seems they will stop at nothing to achieve their ends."

"Quinton, there was a time when I'd be intrigued but not now. But to get back to my visit, it is to give you this. It's the only copy as the negatives have been destroyed."

It was quite late when Obbs said his goodbyes to Peter.

"Now you're sure you won't stay the night? Leave after breakfast?"

"No thanks, Quinton. You forget I have a young son waiting for me at home."

"Oh of course. Thanks again, Peter. Let's hope that one day when you are settled we can have that drink together and all this will seem like a bad dream."

***

"Hello," said Obbs. "I would like to speak to Inspector Wallace, please."

"I am sorry to have to tell you, but the Inspector is in hospital."

"Hospital? Which hospital?"

"The Queen's Hospital in Watford."

"What's the trouble?"

"I'm sorry, sir. May I have your name?"

Obbs put down the phone.

"Betty, Wallace is in hospital."

"What's wrong with him?"

"I don't know. She wanted my name so I rang off. He is in the Queen's in Watford. I'm going there now."

At the hospital, Obbs was told that Wallace was out of Intensive Care and now in Christopher Ward.

He was shocked at how thin and ill Wallace looked.

"Hello old chap, what have you been up to?"

A few moments passed before Wallace recognised his visitor. With that the nurse arrived at his bedside and said, "Now now, Mr Wallace, no-one's going to poison you." She then rolled up his sleeve to give him an injection.

"Are you a relative?" she asked Obbs.

"No, a friend."

"He's been very ill. I'm pleased to say he has got over the worst. I shouldn't stay long – he is still very weak."

Obbs was about to leave when Wallace once again recognised him.

"They took the photo," he said, then fell into a deep sleep.

Eight Years Later

16th June, 1993

The arrival of Betty caused the many different types of birds feeding on the lawn to disappear into the trees and bushes.

"Coffee time, Quinse."

"Sorry dear, I keep dropping off."

"How long is it since you last saw Inspector Wallace?"

"Must be seven or eight years. Why?"

"There's an article in this morning's paper about—" she hesitated for a moment "—Thomas Fairfield's appeal."

He quickly took the newspaper and began to read.

"He's got as much chance of a retrial as I've got of returning to the bar," he said.

"Now, dear, don't upset yourself on this beautiful sunny morning. Don't forget we agreed to put that sordid part of our lives behind us."

"I'm sorry, dear, you are right."

She opened her eyes, glanced at her watch and realised they had both as, Quinse would say, dropped off. She gathered up the cups. Obbs, with one eye open, watched her make her way back into the house before reaching for the newspaper. He quickly put the paper down as Betty approached and sat down beside him. There was no conversation, they just sat there enjoying the sun until she said, "You say it's eight years since you saw Wallace? Good God, how time flies. What happened to him after he came out of hospital?"

"He went back to work for a year or so but had to retire on health grounds. He was convinced, as I was, that Thomas was innocent. He never gave up even after Thomas was found guilty."

With Jill, Roger packed and locked the car then followed the sign to the garden, which was quite a large area with tables and chairs.

"Are you sure this is the pub, Jill?"

"Yes, this is the one, Roger."

There were several small craft tied up alongside the jetty, one or two children with fishing nets and plenty of swans. They had not been seated long before the landlord approached.

"Now what can I get you two on this fine morning?"

"A pint of your best beer and a white wine – and one for yourself, landlord."

"Er, that be very kind of you, sir."

I watched him walk away.

"Rather a large jolly-faced man – I'd say he was from Devon, do you agree, Roger?"

"Yes, I think you are right."

Although it was early October there was still a comfortable warmth from the sun as it shone through the passing clouds.

"It's hard to believe it all started from here," I said, watching Roger fumbling in his pocket and taking a photo of his father from his wallet. He had that same hopeless look on his face that I had seen so many times before. I knew Roger's next move would be to confront the landlord. I could see the landlord, hear his laughter and the occasional word as he served at the tables. I watched him collecting the empty glasses, then he put the tray on our table and gathered up Roger's empty glass.

"Landlord—"

"Call me Bill, sir, most of my customers call me Bill."

"Bill, I know you're busy but could you spare me a few minutes of your time?"

"Of course sir, I'll take these inside and be back in a jiffy."

He sat at the table. "Now, sir, what can I do for you?"

"Do you recognise the man in this photo?"

"Indeed I do, sir. Oh yes, that was the gentleman who had his coat stolen. In fact he was sitting at this very table. He took his coat off as it was so hot that day and hung it on the back of his chair, then came inside for another drink. When he returned it had gone. I rang the police and he then left with two men who I thought were the police but that turned out not to be the case, because the police arrived twenty minutes after he'd left. They asked me why he had left before they arrived and I told them I assumed the two men he'd left with were the police, but perhaps they were friends of his. I did mention about the drunk. We've had a drunk pestering people for drinks – he could have been the thief. He was here that day although I've not seen him since. The gentleman in this photo – is that your father?"

"Yes."

"I thought so, could see the likeness. I'm sorry I could not be more helpful."

I watched him walk away, then disappear inside the Riverside Inn. My thoughts went back to the mortuary. The drunk – it must have been him. Who were the two men with Roger's father? My thoughts were then interrupted.

"At least someone saw Dad on that day, Jill," said Roger.

"Roger, look!"

Turning his head, he could see the landlord pointing out our table. Two rather well-built men approached.

"Do you mind if we join you? Are you Roger Baker?"

I felt a cold, frightening chill as they sat down.

Before Roger could answer, one said, "It's about your father, Roger. He's alive and well."

"Oh thank God. Where is he? Tell me, who are you and how do I know you're telling me the truth?"

"You don't, that's why we want you both to come with us."

With that, both men identified themselves as secret agents working for the Government.

"How did you know we were here?"

"It's been our job to keep an eye on you two. Now are you coming with us or not?"

I could see the concern on the landlord's face.

"Is everything alright, sir?" he asked.

"Yes, thank you, Bill. Thanks for coming over."

Bill waved. I waved back then hurried to catch them up as they made their way to the carpark.

"Oh no, I don't believe it, Jill – the car, it's gone."

"You'll be travelling with us, Mr Baker. Don't worry, your car is in safe hands. It's best you don't know where we are going."

They travelled in silence until one of the men asked, "You two at the back, are you OK?"

"Yes, fine. How much further?"

"Don't worry, we are nearly there."

I was worried. They had left the motorway and were travelling along a tree-lined country lane. I looked at my watch; it had been two hours since we had left the Riverside Inn. Roger squeezed my hand and smiled. Poor Roger, would he see his father, or was this the start of another nightmare?

The car turned off the country lane onto a bumpy track, shuddering as it drove over a cattle grid. I could see in the distance an old country house. The car stopped; so did the noise made by the gravel path. Roger took my arm, helping me alight and by nodding his head drew my attention to my car parked lower down the drive. Four steps and we found ourselves in front of a large oak door. A few moments after our escort rang the bell, the great oak door opened slowly revealing a small middle-aged pleasant-faced lady.

"Good afternoon, sir," she said, smiling as I walked past her. The anxiety and fear I had felt seemed to melt away.

We followed the two men along the corridor and were beckoned into a nicely furnished room.

"Now make yourselves comfortable. Tea or coffee?"

Roger said, "My father. I'd like to see my father."

"He should be here in about two hours' time. Now, I've been instructed before your father's arrival to tell you both the whole story, starting with Gloria Fairfield's murder. Gloria Fairfield was quite a remarkable woman, clever and very beautiful. She liked men and the good things in life. It came to the Government's notice that one of her associates was Boris Kolvolsky, a Russian agent. At that time she was a single woman called Gloria Lavenia with an English mother and Spanish father. She had applied for British Citizenship, which was granted on condition she worked for the Government. It worked well for a time. Agents around the country were located at a price but her parties and drinking became a worry. She was a risk the Government could not take. She disappeared from the scene for several years and it was then that we got involved. She met and married Thomas Fairfield. He was madly in love with her but he knew nothing of her past life. The marriage worked for a time until she got restless. His work took him away from home on several occasions, for days, sometimes weeks. She drifted back to her old ways. When she took up again with Boris Kolvolsky we had her watched. Not only Boris but several rich and influential people paid her a visit.

"Unfortunately, when she was murdered, the police – namely Inspector Wallace – discovered our man opposite who was on surveillance. When asked, he gave the camera and films to the young constable thinking he was sent by us. When it became a police murder enquiry and Thomas Fairfield was arrested and charged with murder, it seemed to be an open-and-shut case and our assignment was finished – or so we thought.

"We were later contacted by our photographer, requesting an urgent meeting, He told us the last person he photographed leaving the house on the day of the murder was none other than a member of the Royal Household. Now we only had his word for that, but could you imagine what problems a photo like that would cause in the wrong hands? Finding Thomas Fairfield guilty of his wife's murder was essential to lessen the importance of the photo. Thomas Fairfield was guilty – no doubt about that – but his barrister at the time was Quinton Obbs and he had other ideas, which would have meant a lengthy trial. Pressure was put on Quinton by Inspector Wallace."

Roger broke his silence, "By pressure, you ruined a man's career and nearly killed another."

"We knew of your visit to Quinton Obbs, Roger, believe me we had no part in that. Our job was to find and destroy that photo."

I realised the pieces were fitting together like a jigsaw, although pieces were still missing. Slowly a picture was beginning to take shape.

It was at that point that an elderly gentleman entered the room.

"The car has arrived, sir."

Roger was on his feet in no time.

"Is he here? My father?"

"Yes, Roger, he has no idea that you are here. He knows you are in England and that you are in good health. He's looking forward to seeing you both, as I know you are longing to see him, but before your reunion I insist that you first understand our reason for keeping your father as we did. It wasn't until your father got interested in the Gloria Fairfield murder again that we got involved. We knew about this meeting at the Riverside Inn. Our CIA friends in America alerted us to a possible kidnap by foreign agents. They, like ourselves, were still interested in the photo he kept at that meeting. Like your father, we have no idea who that was. We know it wasn't the person who stole his coat – apparently that was the local drunk. Whether he was pushed or stumbled into the river, we don't know. The local police identified the victim as your father.

"Do you remember, Miss Bennett, that morning you arrived at your office and found the place ransacked? I can assure you it wasn't burglars. They were hoping to find that photo. Now, Roger, before you meet your father is there anything you would like to ask me?"

"This photo – does it exist? Is it still going to cause more intrigue?"

"No, I think not, with the change of power and the KGB no longer in existence. As for whether it still exists, who knows? Your guess is as good as mine. Now, Roger, the moment you have been waiting for."

Both men embraced each other, tears streaming down their faces, until Roger's father beckoned me over with an outstretched hand, to join them. No words were spoken, just three people locked together enjoying a great moment.

**

Later at Jill's house, standing there in the front porch, they could hear the thunder and see the lightning flashes that followed.

"Thanks for a wonderful evening, Jill. Are you sure you don't want me to wash up or something?"

"No thanks, Roger." I kissed him on the cheek. "It's late. Your Dad looked quite tired."

"Jill, it's years since Dad laughed like he did tonight. Look – they are still laughing," he said looking at Jill's mum and Roger's dad standing by the car.

"Come on, son," said Peter.

I watched Roger walk down the path to the waiting car, wave and drive off. I waited for my mother to join me at the porch.

"Don't forget to lock up, Jill," said mother.

I watched my mother slowly climb the stairs, stopping halfway to say, "Roger's dad, Peter…"

The silence that followed was broken by me saying, "You've taken a shine to him, Mother."

"Oh, go on with you, Jill. Goodnight. See you tomorrow."

I knew sleep wouldn't come easy after the excitement of today. I could hear the wind blowing the leaves on the trees and see the shadows dancing on the ceiling. It was hard to believe so many weeks had passed since Roger was reunited with his father. So much had happened. I could hear Roger's dad saying 'let's have a holiday' and hear the sound of my mother's laughter. How my friendship with Roger had turned to love. The coming months would be busy ones, having decided with Roger to emigrate to Australia. My thoughts were disrupted by a loud clap of thunder. The lightning that followed lit every corner of her bedroom. I lay there listening to the rain beating against the window. I closed my eyes to savour that moment today when Roger kneeling down in front of me said, "Jill, will you marry me?"

Melbourne, Australia

"One egg or two?"

"Two please, Jill."

"What else does he say?"

"Your mother sends her love. They enjoyed themselves in Scotland apart from the rain. According to Dad, it never stopped. Your mother thanks you for her birthday card. They're both looking forward to September and so am I. It will be nice to see them both. There's a 'PS'. Hello what's this?"

I placed his breakfast on the table in front of him.

"What's what?"

"Apparently Dad's been invited, along with Wallace and Obbs, by Thomas Fairfield…."

"Oh no, Roger not again."

"Hang on, Jill." Roger continued to read on before saying, "According to this, it seems he wants to celebrate his first year of freedom by inviting the three of them to a celebration party. It's his way of saying thank you for the part they played during the trial, If I remember it rightly it was Wallace who played a big part in his release. Dad never believed him guilty. Remember Quinton Obbs, dear? All three thought him innocent."

"I don't want to remember, Roger. What else do they say?"

"Apparently Dad has accepted. He said he's looking forward to seeing his old friends again."

Roger wasn't the only one interested in a letter. Back home in England, his father once again sat down to read:

Mr Baker,

I left instructions that you were to receive this letter after my death. Sorry we never kept our appointment at the Riverside Inn. I did turn up, but late owing to an accident, only to see you leaving with two men. Then I believed it to be you found drowned, as reported in the local paper.

I've realised since that I was wrong trying to extort money from you. I should have gone to the police. At least this letter will put your mind at rest.

On the morning Gloria Fairfield was murdered, I had a call to pick up a Mr Jones on the corner of Ash Lane. For a man so well dressed, I was surprised when he said he wanted to go to Potter Shopping Centre. He was gone about thirty minutes and when he returned had no shopping and he looked terrible. I asked him whether he was alright and he said, "I am now, driver." I drove him back to Ash Lane; his hands were trembling as he fumbled to pay his fare. I was curious, so I parked around the corner, walked to the end of the road and watched him get into a car and drive off.

A few days later, I saw a photograph in the newspaper showing Mr Jones to be Thomas Fairfield, wanted for his wife's murder.

So there you are, Mr Baker, as they say. The ball is in your court.

Yours sincerely,

Alan Dates.

***

"You're quiet tonight, dear – anything wrong?"

"Yes, I am thinking about tomorrow," said Peter. "Actually I'm not looking forward to it."

"Oh you do surprise me. I thought you were looking forward to meeting your old friends."

"I was until I received a letter concerning our host. It puts me in a rather awkward position. I realise I must do something, but what?"

"Is it that serious?"

"Yes, I'm afraid it is. I now have in my possession written evidence that suggests justice was not done."

***

The next morning he once again glanced at his invitation:

> Dear Mr Baker,
>
> It would give me great pleasure if you would join me with your old associates —

At that point he was interrupted by the ringing of the phone.

"Hello, Quinton, how are you? Is it that long ago? Yes, just about to leave. I too was surprised by our invitation. Yes, Wallace is going. He declined my offer of a lift. Said he'd made arrangements to call in on a relative on his way down. And you. Safe journey. See you later."

The Drive

Each passing mile brought him nearer. He had to make a decision. Should he mention the letter to Wallace and Obbs and confront their host with this accusation? All these things were going through his mind. Should he tear the letter up? Why start getting involved again? The truth, he had to know the truth.

There were two cars on the driveway when he arrived. He came to a stop, felt inside his jacket pocket, knowing full well how this letter would be received. How could he enjoy the spirit of the evening knowing that sometime—

"Another brandy, Peter?" Before he could answer, Thomas Fairfield was refilling his glass.

"You alright, old chap?"

"Not really, Thomas."

"Gentlemen, may I have your attention?" asked Peter.

Wallace retrieved his glass, fully expecting to toast their host. Peter waited for a moment or two before saying, "A letter has come into my possession which concerns us all. I have no reason but to believe it's authentic." He ignored the outstretched hand of Thomas Fairfield. "Quinton, would you be so kind?" Obbs took the letter and started to read but never said a word until, "Good God. Do you realise what this means?" He then handed the letter to Wallace.

Peter could not help noticing how white Wallace had turned whilst reading the letter.

"Why should we believe this?" asked Wallace.

The three men stood in silence while Thomas read the letter. He smiled then handed the letter back to Peter, before saying, "Well, gentleman, what do you intend to do now?"

"Is it true?" asked Obbs. "This letter implies that you returned home before your journey to Newcastle. Why? Did you kill your wife?" The tone of his voice when saying *'Did you kill your wife?'* reminded Peter of those early trial days; he still had that command.

Obbs continued, "Three people's lives were ruined the day your wife was murdered. I know mine was, also Inspector Wallace's and to a lesser extent Peter's. All three of us became involved one way or another, so let's use this evening to put the record straight."

Thomas refilled his brandy glass before saying, "Gentlemen, to put the record straight I must start at the beginning. I fell in love with Gloria the moment I saw her. She had many admirers that evening and I felt flattered that she spent the evening with me. I saw her as often as I could, neglecting my business to be with her. I proposed and she accepted. She had extravagant tastes and spent money like water. I found myself working round the clock, travelling around the country and away from home for long periods. She got bored, it was a mistake, she had no time for me.

"I can still see her now, standing there waving to me. I watched her in my side window as I drove away. I'd known for a long time of Paul's affair with Gloria and the Claremont Hotel meetings. He always needed a few days off when Gloria was visiting her aunt. Her shameless affairs – how humiliated I felt.

"Driving to the office on that Monday morning I asked myself why; I'd given her everything. With Paul's 'pleasant journey, Thomas' ringing in my ears, I parked the car a mile or so from the office and rang for a taxi. I told the cabbie I would be about half an hour in the supermarket. I entered and then left by the back door and went back to the house. I quietly turned the key in the door and could hear laughter coming from the upstairs bedroom. I just managed to hide myself in the downstairs cupboard when I heard him say 'Don't worry, Gloria, I'll let myself out'. Climbing the stairs, I opened the bedroom door; lying the way she was on the bed, Gloria never saw me enter. 'You've forgotten something' she said and these were her last words as I tightened my grip around her throat.

"My hand was trembling as I fumbled for the notes in my wallet to pay the cabbie. I made a point of saying 'I hate shopping' to him and told him to drop me off at the same place where he had picked me up. Paid the cab driver and waited until he'd gone out of sight, then walked to my car. I felt cold and my hands were still trembling but I felt sure everything had gone to plan… until this evening. I'm not a violent man and I am sorry for what I have done, but at that time my love had turned to hatred. I gave her everything and she gave me nothing."

He then finished his brandy and placed his glass on the table.

"I thought you were innocent of the crime. We all did. How could we be so wrong?" said Obbs.

"I thought I *was* innocent. It was only when I picked up a paper from a park seat whilst recovering from my car accident and saw my photo with the heading 'Thomas Fairfield wanted for killing his wife'. My name, where I was, how I got there – I had no idea. I had no memory of anything. It took months before things began to fit together, months during which time you three convinced me I was innocent and my release was only a matter of time. It was then that my case took a turn for the worse. New barrister, new Police Inspector – I'm found guilty and sentenced. If it had not been for Wallace here, I'd still be there now. He came to see me, knowing I'd been granted a retrial. He was a shadow of the man I first knew. He told me how ill he'd been. I asked him 'My retrial! What are my chances, Wallace?' He made it clear to me that I had no chance as my retrial was just a formality. They had no intention of setting me free, but why? Wallace knew the reason why—" He lowered his voice, "—he said he had in his possession the key to my release. I should tell my barrister that I knew about the photo, and at my trial I would identify the person. He said I needed to know no more. I was granted a pardon on lack of evidence.

"I wanted to thank Wallace and I wanted to know more about that photo. Eventually I traced him to a bedsit in Hammersmith. Do you remember what you said on my leaving? Forget about that photo – it's best you know nothing. Anyway, I felt I had to do something. He needed some fresh air and sunshine so I bought him Dove Cottage. Gentlemen, it is for you to decide. You can destroy this letter or use it to prove my guilt."

71

He finished his brandy and left the room.

They listened in silence, hardly believing what he was saying. How could they have been so wrong? The man who they believed had suffered a great miscarriage of justice, this man was a murderer.

"Should I have ignored this letter?" asked Peter. "Obbs, what do we do, now we know the truth? We can destroy this letter or give it to the authorities and let justice take its course."

"Justice?" replied Obbs, "There's been no justice. From the very beginning they spent more time looking for that bloody photo than trying to find the murderer. There's always been someone trying to get their hands on that photo and all the time Wallace had it."

"I haven't got the photo. I've never had the photo. I gave Fairfield the key to freedom and he gave you Dove Cottage."

Thomas Fairfield entered the room and said, "No it wasn't like that. He knew nothing about the cottage – that was my idea."

The long silence was broken by Peter Baker saying he was off to Australia tomorrow.

"I'm not cancelling that," he said, "whatever we decide. I know how important this is, but so is seeing my son."

"Look, we don't have to come to a decision this evening," said Obbs. "We need time to think this over. Let's leave it until you return from Australia."

Little did they know this would be their last meeting.

***

Sitting there, it was hard to realise they had been back a month from Australia.

"I'm going to make a coffee, Peter."

He watched her make her way back into the house. Leaning back and closing his eyes, his thoughts returned back to the reunion. He wasn't looking forward to the problem he left behind, but was pleased that he had kept this affair to himself. There was no way he was going to involve Roger and Jill. That bloody letter!

Tragic Events

"Hello, could I speak to Quinton, please. It's Peter Baker here."

"I'm afraid Mrs Obbs isn't available at the moment and I assume you don't know about Mr Obbs, sir? I'm sorry to say he is no longer with us; he passed away last month with suspected food poisoning."

After a long silence she added, "Hello, are you still there?"

"Oh I'm sorry, it's the shock," said Peter, having composed himself somewhat. "I would be grateful if you would be kind enough to pass my sincere condolences on to Mrs Obbs."

He put the phone down, hardly believing the news.

"Is everything alright, Peter?"

"It's Quinton – he is dead."

He couldn't leave it much longer; he had to call on Wallace. It was a beautiful morning, cold but sunny with a slight breeze, so he wasn't prepared for his next shock. As he turned the corner he saw a sign that read 'Dove Cottage – For Sale'. He made his way up the garden path and knocked on the door.

A neighbour called out, "Can I help you?"

"I'm trying to contact Mr Wallace."

"Are you a relative?"

"No, a friend."

"You must prepare yourself for a shock. Mr Wallace committed suicide by gassing himself."

"Gassed himself? I don't believe it. When?"

"Two weeks ago today. We had no idea, as he kept himself to himself. I was speaking to him in the morning over the garden fence. I thought he'd be the last person to take his own life."

"I take it the police were involved."

"Yes, I rang the police the next morning. There was his newspaper still in the door and a strong smell of gas. When the police arrived they had to force the front door, but there was nothing they could do."

"Can you remember, did he have any visitors that day?"

"Not as far as we know, although the wife did hear a car drive away in the early hours of the morning. Look, I can see how upset you are. Why don't you come in for a moment or two?"

The neighbour was joined at that point by his wife who said, "Oh, there you are."

"I was telling er—"

Peter interrupted, "Peter Baker."

"—Mr Baker about our neighbour. So sad; such a nice man. I still can't believe it."

Having thanked them and said his goodbyes, Peter left.

With Obbs and Wallace gone, he was alone now and found himself having to decide Thomas Fairfield's fate. All these thoughts were passing through his mind as he made his way home.

It was all in the letter. He'd wait for a reply but should he not receive one by the 25th of October, there would be no alternative than to go to the police with the letter he'd received from Alan Dates, as he no longer wanted anything more to do with the whole affair.

∗∗∗

It was week later, and they had enjoyed their meal together, but during coffee Jill's mother said, "Peter, there's something that's been worrying you. Your thoughts have been miles away. Is there anything you'd like to tell me? You've been so quiet since we've been home from Australia."

"I didn't want you to worry, Mary. I was to arrange a meeting with Obbs and Wallace on my return but I'm afraid that's impossible now."

"How strange, Peter, that both men died in such a short time."

"Yes, Mary, very strange. I was expecting a reply to a letter I sent which hasn't arrived so it's left to me to do what I am sure Wallace and Obbs would agree with."

"What's that?"

"To bring a man to justice."

How long she'd been standing in the front porch waiting for their arrival I had no idea until I said, "It's me, Mum."

"Jill, oh Jill!" With tears running down her face, she said again, "Oh, Jill!"

Roger soon joined them and cradled them both in his arms.

"Let's go inside, mother."

I watched my mother's tears streaming down her face while she tried so hard to drink her tea. There was nothing I could say to lessen my mother's sadness, or the sadness and the tears I'd seen on Roger's face the day he read the telegram.

"Sorry we were so late, Mother, our flight was delayed."

Roger waited until he felt Mary had regained her composure before saying, "What day is the funeral, Mary?"

"Thursday. One-thirty at the Memory Lane Church." Once again tears began to fill her eyes. "It was a hit and run."

"Have they arrested anyone?"

"No, Roger. A young boy delivering newspapers noticed a man standing over him. The boy thought he saw him take something from his pocket, then get in his car and drive off."

"Did he get the number plate?"

"No, unfortunately. The police have appealed to anyone who might have witnessed the accident to come forward."

***

I squeezed his hand as we watched the coffin being slowly lowered into the grave. Ashes to ashes, dust to dust. No longer could Roger hide his grief as the tears ran down his face. I turned and grabbed my mother's arm, saying, "See you at the car, Roger," knowing he wanted those last moments alone. He'd never felt such sadness in his life before, never would he shake his father's hand again or relive times gone by. He suddenly felt cold and dizzy. The journey, the anxiety, the lack of food, were catching up with him. It was then he felt a hand on his shoulder.

"Are you alright, young man?"

Roger quickly wiped the tears from his eyes.

"Yes, thanks."

"Your father?" he asked. Roger could only nod his head. "Oh, I'm sorry. Are you sure you're alright now?"

"Yes, I feel much better now, thank you."

The man began to walk away when Roger said, "And who do I owe this kindness to?"

He turned and said, *"Thomas Fairfield."*